WITHDRAWN

THE ZACK FILES™

Greenish Eggs and Dinosaurs

LETTERS TO DAN GREENBURG
ABOUT THE ZACK FILES:

From a mother in New York, NY: "Just wanted to let you know that it was THE ZACK FILES that made my son discover the joy of reading...I tried everything to get him interested...THE ZACK FILES turned my son into a reader overnight. Now he complains when he's out of books!"

From a boy named Toby in New York, NY: "The reason why I like your books is because you explain things that no other writer would even dream of explaining to kids."

From Tara in Floral Park, NY: "When I read your books I felt like I was in the book with you. We love your books!"

From a teacher in West Chester, PA: "I cannot thank you enough for writing such a fantastic series."

From Max in Old Bridge, NJ: "I wasn't such a great reader until I discovered your books."

From Monica in Burbank, IL: "I read almost all of your books and I loved the ones I read. I'm a big fan! *I'm Out of My Body, Please Leave a Message*. That's a funny title. It makes me think of it being the best book in the world."

From three mothers in Toronto: "You have managed to take three boys and unlock the world of reading. In January they could best be characterized as boys who 'read only under duress.' Now these same guys are similar in that they are motivated to READ."

From Stephanie in Hastings, NY: "If someone didn't like your books that would be crazy."

From Dana in Floral Park, NY: "I really LOVE I mean LOVE your books. I read them a million times. I wish I could buy more. They are so good and so funny."

From a teacher in Pelham, NH: "My students are thoroughly enjoying [THE ZACK FILES]. Some are reading a book a night."

From Madeleine in Hastings, NY: "I love your books...I hope you keep making many more Zack Files."

THE ZACK FILES™

Greenish Eggs and Dinosaurs

By Dan Greenburg

Illustrated by Jack E. Davis

GROSSET & DUNLAP • NEW YORK

For Judith, and for the real Zack,
with love—D.G.

I'd like to thank my editor
Jane O'Connor, who makes the process
of writing and revising so much fun,
and without whom
these books would not exist.

I also want to thank
Emily Sollinger and Tui Sutherland
for their terrific ideas.

Text copyright © 2001 by Dan Greenburg. Illustrations copyright © 2001 by Jack E. Davis.
All rights reserved. Published by Grosset & Dunlap, a division of Penguin Putnam Books
for Young Readers, New York. GROSSET & DUNLAP and THE ZACK FILES are trademarks
of Penguin Putnam Inc. Published simultaneously in Canada. Printed in the U.S.A.

Library of Congress Cataloging-in-Publication Data is available.

ISBN 0-448-42546-7   A B C D E F G H I J

Chapter 1

I've always loved dinosaurs, but it turns out they make really lousy pets. Perhaps I should explain.

My name is Zack. I'm ten and a half and I'm in the fifth grade at the Horace Hyde-White School for Boys in New York City. My parents are divorced, and I live half the time with my dad.

The thing I want to tell you about started one Sunday afternoon at an outdoor flea market that's near Dad's apartment.

They don't sell fleas there, in case you were wondering. They sell just about everything else, though. The last time I went there I bought a strange brass box from a little old man from Tibet. It made lots of clones of me. It made so many clones of me that Dad's apartment was crawling with little Zacks. But that's a whole other story.

Anyway, I went back to the flea market because I was looking for a birthday present for my dad. Probably because it was a Sunday, the flea market was really crowded. There were amazing things on sale there. Giant pink plastic flamingos to put on your lawn. Hula hoops. Snow tires. Toilets used as planters. And something that looked really interesting—a huge green egg resting on a little stand. I thought it might be an ostrich egg, but it looked a lot bigger than that. Also, I don't remember ostrich eggs being green. I carefully picked

up the egg. It weighed around ten pounds. I'm not kidding you.

"You drop him, you bought him," said this high, crackly voice in back of me.

That startled me so badly I almost dropped the egg. Holding it carefully, I turned around. A tiny old man was grinning at me. His face was very tan, and as wrinkled as an elephant's. His bald head was as smooth and shiny as an eggplant. He was dressed in long, faded orange robes. Peeking out from underneath his robes were red high-top sneakers. It was the same old guy who'd sold me the brass box that cloned me.

"Hello again, young gentlemans," said the old man. "You like make big omelette?" He giggled like crazy.

"What kind of egg is this, sir?" I asked. "Ostrich?"

"No ostrich," said the old man. "Better than ostrich. Much better." He winked at me.

"What, then?" I said.

He motioned for me to lean closer. When I did he grabbed my ear and whispered into it: "Two words: Dino…saur."

"You're telling me this is the egg of a dinosaur?"

"Ssshhh! Please! Not want whole flea market to hear."

"Where'd you get it?"

"Tibet. You like to buy him? I make special price for young gentlemans. Six thousand dollar."

"Six thousand dollars! I don't have anywhere near six thousand dollars!"

"OK. Give me thirty dollar, he's yours."

"I don't even have thirty."

"How much you got?"

I emptied my pockets and looked at the crumpled ball of bills and coins in my hand.

"I've got twelve dollars and sixty-seven cents."

"OK," he said. He snatched the money out of my hand. "I wrap him up for you."

He took the egg out of my hands and started wrapping it up.

"Wait a minute," I said. "I don't know if I even want this thing. I mean, how do I know it's a real dinosaur egg?"

"Tell me something. Did brass box I sell you make clones?"

"Yeah, I guess so."

"So," he giggled. "You satisfied customer?"

I didn't want to get into that. It had been a disaster.

He finished wrapping the egg and handed it back to me.

"Whatever you do," he said, "don't put him in microwave oven. Dinosaurs *hate* microwave ovens."

Chapter 2

"Happy birthday, Dad," I said.

Dad unwrapped my present. He looked puzzled.

"Thanks, Zack. It's, uh, just what I always wanted."

"Do you know what it is?"

"Uh, let me guess. An egg?"

"Yes, but what *kind* of egg?"

"Ostrich?"

"Nope. Dinosaur."

"Uh-huh. Well, thanks very much, Zack. I appreciate it."

"You don't believe it's a dinosaur egg, do you?" I asked.

"Well, frankly, no. I'm afraid I don't."

"Dad, the little old Tibetan guy who sold it to me? He's the same guy who sold me the box that made clones of me. The box was real, so I figured this might be, too."

"I see."

"You hate it, don't you?" I said.

"Hate it? No, not at all," he said. "I like it. I really do. As a matter of fact, I've always wanted a...very large green egg. I think it'll really come in handy."

"OK," I said. "Tomorrow I'll take it back and get you something else."

"No, Zack," said Dad. He could tell I was hurt. "I'm starting to like it. It's beginning to grow on me, you know? I'm liking it more already."

"Whatever," I said.

He looked at it closely.

"This thing is really filthy," he said.

"Well, it *is* over a hundred million years old," I pointed out.

"Veroushka will know what to do with it," said Dad.

"Veroushka?" I said.

"The new housekeeper I hired. She's supposed to be a fantastic worker. My editor at *Wool World* gave me her number. He said two bachelors like us need somebody to do a little straightening up around here, and maybe cook us a meal or two. He's right. Anyway, she starts tomorrow."

I nodded, but I wasn't really listening. I was looking at the egg. Tomorrow, I thought to myself, I'll take it back to the guy at the flea market and get Dad something he'll really like.

If I knew then what I know now, I wouldn't have waited till tomorrow. I wouldn't have waited even another minute.

Chapter 3

The doorbell rang the next morning at seven sharp. Dad and I were both asleep. It was a school holiday—Teacher Relaxation day, I think. I staggered to the door and opened it. There stood one of the most beautiful women I've ever seen. She was carrying a mop and a shopping bag full of cleaning stuff.

"I am Veroushka!" she said. She spoke pretty loudly for seven in the morning.

"I am Zack," I said.

"Howdy-doody, Zack!" she said. She

grabbed my hand hard and pumped it up and down.

Dad staggered into the room, saw Veroushka, and perked right up.

"Howdy-doody, I am Veroushka!" she said. "I come too early?"

"No no, not at all," said Dad, combing his hair with his fingers. "I'm Dan."

Veroushka grabbed Dad's hand and pumped it up and down.

"I am please to meeting you!" she said.

"Me too," said Dad. "Veroushka, why don't you get started in the kitchen. You can wash the dishes in the sink, and clean up the stove for starters. Then maybe you can fix us both a little something to eat."

"Okel-dokel!" she said. She went into the kitchen.

"Oh, and Veroushka, could you please do something with that egg on the counter?" Dad called.

"Okel-dokel!" she called back.

I was getting dressed after my shower when I heard an explosion. It sounded like a cherry bomb had gone off in the kitchen. I rushed in to see if Veroushka was all right.

As I walked into the kitchen, showers of sparks shot out of the back of the microwave. A cloud of green smoke poured out of it. Then a smell like rotting pumpkins filled the room. From somewhere I heard what sounded like a tiny scream.

Veroushka was standing there looking terrified. Dad walked in.

"Veroushka, what happened?" he asked.

"I not know," she said. "I so sorry."

Dad opened the microwave door and looked inside. More green smoke poured out, and the smell of rotting pumpkins got worse. I looked inside the microwave. There was the egg. I expected there to be green yuck all over the place, but except for a

small crack at the top, the egg looked fine. Well, not exactly fine. The egg was glowing with a weird green glow.

"You put the egg in the *microwave*?" I said. "That was the one thing that the flea market guy said *not* to do!"

Veroushka shrugged. "I want make nice breakfast for you and your dad. I so sorry. I spoiling your breakfast."

Oh boy! I had a feeling that we had a bigger problem on our hands than break-fast. She started to take the egg, but stopped when she burned her fingers.

"Whew! Still hotsy-totsy!" she said.

She pulled on an oven mitt and took the egg out of the microwave. A thin wisp of green smoke curled out of the top of the egg. Just then I heard a soft popping sound. The crack at the top of the egg grew longer.

"Uh-oh," said Veroushka.

Another soft popping sound. Another crack grew out from the first crack. Then a whole bunch of cracks spread over the egg like a spider web.

"Something is happening," I whispered.

There was a tapping sound from inside the egg.

"Did you hear that?" I said. "There's something *alive* inside that thing!"

"Nonsense," said Dad. "Nothing could survive being cooked in the microwave."

The tapping sound got louder. Then the entire top of the egg popped off it. Something green and slimy poked its head out and looked at us with glowing red eyes.

It had a long pointed snout, and when it opened its mouth I saw rows of sharp, tiny teeth. Its skin was scaly and slimy and green.

"Holy guacamole!" I said. "A dinosaur!"

Chapter 4

The funny thing is, the little guy was almost cute. In a red-eyed, slimy, jagged-toothed kind of way, I mean.

"Dinosaurs have been extinct for about sixty-five million years," said Dad. "This is not a dinosaur. This is a baby iguana."

"He very cute," said Veroushka.

Whatever it was made a sound like a crow and broke through the rest of the shell. It was the weirdest animal I'd ever seen. It had a long snake-like neck, a humped back, a tail, and four diamond-shaped flippers. It was about a foot long.

Dad stared at it like he was in a trance. It turned to me and rubbed its head against my hand, just like a pussycat. Only slimier.

"Can we keep it, Dad?" I asked. "It would be such a great pet."

"No more pets," said Dad. "Every goldfish we've owned died and had to be flushed down the toilet. Then there was the plan to get a kitten, which resulted in—"

"—my getting a big tomcat who was my reincarnated great-grandfather Maurice," I said. "I know that, Dad, but—"

"Then we had that terrible experience with the baby boa constrictor. And the baby vulture. And the tarantula Mrs. Coleman-Levin had you keep over spring vacation. Which ended up with—"

"—nobody on our floor ever speaking to

us again," I said. "I know that, Dad. But if you let us keep this baby dinosaur, I promise you I'll do all the work. Even though I bought it for you, I'll take care of it and feed it and—"

"If you'll recall," said Dad, "the landlord said that no pets are permitted in the entire building—*especially* not for us. You must get rid of this thing immediately."

The baby dinosaur wriggled over to Veroushka. She backed away. Then it went to Dad and looked up at him with its beady red eyes.

"Dad, he's so cute. See how he's staring at you? He likes you. You know how baby chicks bond to the first animal they see after they hatch because they think it's their mom? That's what he's doing with you, Dad. He thinks you're his mom."

Dad smiled at the baby dinosaur. Then he reached out to pet it. The baby dinosaur opened its mouth and bit down hard on Dad's finger. Dad yelped like a puppy. A little drop of blood oozed out of the end of his finger.

Veroushka screamed.

"Zack, this thing is a menace!" said Dad. "Get rid of it *immediately*!"

My heart sank. When Dad decides something, that's it. And he had clearly decided not to keep our dinosaur.

I looked around for something to carry the dinosaur back to the flea market. On a shelf above the stove was the birdcage we had used for the baby vulture. Well, if it was good enough for the vulture, it was good enough for the dinosaur.

Chapter 5

I never expected the Tibetan guy to get so angry.

"You disobey me!" he screamed at me. "You disobey me! What did I say is the one thing you must never do with dinosaur egg?" He was hopping up and down with anger. People were staring. "What I say to you?" he screamed. "You remember?"

"You said...never put the egg in the microwave," I answered. "I know that, sir. But Veroushka, our new housekeeper, put it in the microwave. It's not my fault."

The baby dinosaur snapped at the old guy's hand through the birdcage. The old guy yanked his hand away.

"Not care whose fault!" he shouted. "Not care who put egg in microwave! What you buy was *egg*. What you try to return now is dinosaur. Cannot return something different from what you buy!"

"Uh huh," I said. 'Well, the thing is, sir, I can't keep this thing. Isn't there some way you could take it and give me back my money?"

The baby dinosaur snapped at the bars of his cage.

"So sorry, but no. No way, José."

———〜———

I left the flea market. I didn't know what to do with the baby dinosaur, but I knew I had to get rid of him. Who might want to buy an unusual reptile? Maybe a zoo. Yes, of course. They'd be thrilled to have him. They might even buy him for more than the twelve dollars and sixty-seven cents that I'd paid for him. I took the baby dinosaur on the bus to the Central Park Zoo on Fifth Avenue. In the zoo office I asked to speak to the head zookeeper. Out came a lady in a tan safari suit and a safari helmet.

"And what have we here?" asked the zookeeper lady.

"He's a baby dinosaur," I said. "I thought the zoo might like to buy him."

The zookeeper lady chuckled. "He does look a tiny bit like a baby dinosaur, doesn't he?" she said. "But dinosaurs, of course, have been extinct for sixty-five million years."

"Except this one," I said. "This is a real dinosaur. He's really valuable."

"If he's so valuable," she said, "then why don't you keep him yourself?"

"Well, our landlord doesn't allow pets. And for another thing..."

Just then the baby dinosaur poked his head out between the bars of the cage and bit the lady on the wrist.

"...for another thing," I said, "he bites."

The zookeeper lady tried to pretend that animal bites didn't bother her. She dabbed at the blood on her wrist with a handkerchief.

"The thing is," she said, "we're really short of space here in our reptile house. Whatever this animal is—and I assure you it's not a dinosaur—we really can't take any more exhibits here. I'm sorry."

Then she steered me out the door.

If the zoo wouldn't take a baby dinosaur, then who would? The only place I'd ever seen a dinosaur was at the Rosencrantz Museum of Natural History. All they had were skeletons. They'd probably be thrilled to get a live one. At a pay phone, I called the Museum. I was connected to Professor Horatio Fufu, the head of New Exhibits. I begged him to see me. He agreed.

I walked across Central Park and took the bus uptown to the Rosencrantz Museum. In the basement of the museum was where they put together the huge dinosaur skeletons. It was also where they arranged the stuffed bodies of dead monkeys, lions, antelopes, and elephants to make up their exhibits. It was kind of a creepy place.

In an office in the museum basement was where I met Professor Fufu. His desk was piled so high with stacks of papers they were spilling onto the floor. Professor Fufu was tall and kind of stooped over. He had brown hair and brown eyes and brown teeth. He was smoking a pipe. Puffs of stinky blue smoke came out of his mouth between sentences.

"How do you do, Professor," I said. "Thanks for seeing me so quickly."

"It's not like I have anything *else* to do," he said.

"You don't?" I said. "I thought you'd be really busy."

"Busy?" said the Professor. "Of *course* I'm busy. Can't you see all these papers on my desk? I'm sure you've never heard of *sarcasm* before. Now what is it you were so anxious to show me?"

"This," I said proudly. I lifted up the birdcage.

"I don't suppose you'd care to inform me what *that* is?"

"Can't you tell?" I said. "It's a baby dinosaur."

"Oh, how could I not have *known* that? How could I have been so *silly*? Wait a minute. Could it be because dinosaurs have been extinct for over sixty-five million years? Could that be it?"

"That must have been it, sir," I said. "Well, now that you know, how'd you like to buy him and display him in your museum?"

The professor burst out laughing. He laughed so hard there were tears in his eyes. I guess he didn't think so much of my idea.

"Professor, this is a dinosaur," I said. "Upstairs you have skeletons of dead ones, and people stand in line for hours to see them. Can you imagine how many people would come to see a *live* one?"

The professor stopped laughing. He wiped the tears from his eyes.

"Is there the *slightest* possibility this creature is a dinosaur? No. But does it look like what a baby *might* have looked like? Perhaps. People might find that interesting. I suppose it wouldn't kill me to give you two hundred dollars for it."

Wow! I only paid twelve dollars and sixty-seven cents for the egg. That's a profit of more than a hundred and eighty dollars! I'd be able to buy Dad a really cool birthday present and have a lot left over.

"Professor, you've got a deal," I said.

I shook his hand. He gave me the two hundred. I gave him the birdcage.

The baby dinosaur cocked his head and looked at me like he knew I was getting rid of him. He seemed sad. I felt awful. Well, maybe I'd come back and visit him here at the museum. Yeah, that's what I'd do. I'd come back here and visit him a lot.

"So tell me, Professor," I said. "How are you going to display him?"

"How do you think? In an exhibit, perhaps?"

"But, I mean...you'll take good care of him, right? Feed him properly?"

"I don't think that will be necessary, my

dear young man." The professor chuckled. "This is the Rosencrantz Museum of Natural History. Look around, please. Do you see any live exhibits here?"

I got a sick feeling in my stomach. "Y-you're going to kill my baby dinosaur?"

"It is no longer *your* anything," said Professor Fufu.

I threw the money at him. "Here's your money," I said. "Give him back."

"I'm afraid it is a little too late for that now, young man. A deal is a deal."

"But I gave you the money back. There's no more deal!"

"You think a deal can be made and unmade like a bed? It cannot. We shook hands. The matter is settled. Good *day*, young man."

He puffed out a huge cloud of blue smoke in my face.

I grabbed for the birdcage. The Professor held on tight. I pulled as hard as I could. He pulled as hard as he could. The baby dinosaur bit him and he let go suddenly. I took the birdcage and ran.

"Stop, thief!" shouted the Professor. "Guards! Stop the thief! He's stealing museum property!"

I ran through the basement. The baby dinosaur started screaming in his cage. A guard came running up.

"Hey, buster!" he said. "Where do you think *you're* going?"

"This is my baby dinosaur, and I'm taking him home!"

"Like heck you are!" said the guard.

He lunged for the birdcage. I tripped him. He fell down. I raced up the stairway to the main floor and out the door before anyone could catch me.

Chapter 6

The next day was Tuesday. I decided to bring the baby dinosaur to school. It had definitely grown bigger overnight. Not knowing what else to feed it, Dad and I gave it a can of salmon and half of a leftover Whopper from Burger King. The baby dinosaur almost didn't fit into the birdcage anymore. As soon as the guys in my homeroom saw it, they all came over to look at it.

"Is that a monitor lizard or a komodo dragon?" asked Spencer. Spencer's my best friend and the smartest kid in my school.

"It's a baby dinosaur, Spencer," I said.

"Amazing," said Spencer. "I was thinking Jurassic, but I wasn't sure."

"I had baby dinosaur twins once," said Andrew Clancy, the kid who always tries to top me. "But I got bored with them and gave them away."

"What did this thing cost?" asked Vernon Manteuffel. His parents are so rich, their weekend house has a game farm with animals on it from Africa.

"It cost twelve dollars and sixty-seven cents," I answered.

"Is that all?" said Vernon. "My folks are buying me a hippopotamus for my birthday. It costs a hundred thousand dollars. I don't even *like* hippos."

"Where would you keep a hippopotamus?" I asked.

"In the servants' pool, I suppose," Vernon said.

"Our servants had a pool," said Andrew. "It was a *wave*-pool. But we got rid of it."

"Why?" I asked.

"They spent too much time surfing and not enough serving," said Andrew. Then he doubled up laughing at his own joke.

Mrs. Coleman-Levin came over and looked at the baby dinosaur. She is our homeroom and science teacher.

"Do you think this is a real dinosaur, Mrs. Coleman-Levin?" I asked.

"Absolutely," she said. "In fact, it's a plesiosaur. A kind of dinosaur that lived in water. Why haven't you put him in water?"

"Who knew I had to?" I said.

"Well, when you get home," said Mrs. Coleman-Levin, "put him in the bathtub. Otherwise his skin will get flaky and peel. You don't want a flaky, peeling plesiosaur, believe me. You know, some marine biologists think the Loch Ness Monster is a plesiosaur like this little fellow here."

"Cool! You mean I have a baby Loch Ness Monster?"

"Perhaps. And creatures who look like this have been spotted in lakes all over the world at the same latitude as Loch Ness. They've been seen in all the Scottish lochs. And in the fjords of Norway. In fact, a creature like this one has been reported living in Upper New York State. In Lake Champlain. They call him Champy." Leave it to Mrs. Coleman-Levin to know all this stuff. She is a very cool teacher.

"Mrs. Coleman-Levin, my dad won't let me keep him at home. I was wondering—could you maybe keep him here?"

"Absolutely not. This type of dinosaur grows very rapidly. Soon he'll be the size of a full-grown alligator. Full grown, he'll be 50 feet long. We just don't have the space."

Chapter 7

Dad wasn't too thrilled to see I still had the dinosaur when I got home.

"I thought you were going to leave him at school," he said.

"I tried to," I said. "But Mrs. Coleman-Levin didn't want him. And she said we had to keep him in the bathtub or his skin will get flaky and peel."

"I will not have my bathtub occupied by a dinosaur," said Dad.

"OK," I said. "You want it to be your fault when his skin starts peeling? You really want a dinosaur with peeling skin on your conscience, Dad?"

Dad sighed. I took the dinosaur into the bathroom. I filled the tub and put him in it. He started paddling around like crazy. He loved it. He was now the size of a Cocker Spaniel. A green, slimy Cocker Spaniel. I still thought he was kind of cute.

I looked around for something to keep him company in the tub. In the bathroom closet I found my old rubber ducky. Dad is kind of mushy about keeping my old baby stuff. When I put the rubber ducky in the tub with the baby dinosaur, he seemed really happy. I kind of wish I hadn't done that now.

Then, during dinner, suddenly there were terrible sounds coming from the bathroom. When I opened the bathroom door, I saw why. The dinosaur had grown. Now he was the size of a small alligator. He'd eaten the rubber ducky, a tube of toothpaste, and both our toothbrushes. He looked at me and hic-cuped. I shut the bathroom door.

"How's he doing in there?" Dad asked.

"Uh, pretty good," I said. "I think he might want more for dinner than a can of salmon and half a Whopper, though."

The dinosaur made a very loud noise. Kind of a roar, actually.

"Did I just hear a roar in there?" Dad asked. "I didn't know he roared."

"Well, I guess he does now," I said.

The dinosaur roared again. A neighbor banged on the wall.

"That was definitely a roar," said Dad.

The dinosaur roared so loudly, the plates on our dinner table rattled. Two neighbors called up to complain about the noise. I can't say I blamed them.

"We can't have this roaring," said Dad. "This is much too loud."

Dad marched up to the bathroom and

opened the door. I was right behind him. Dad stared into the bathroom. There was another roar, one so loud a large picture fell off the wall and crashed to the floor. Dad closed the bathroom door very quietly.

"Zack, we are in terrible trouble," he whispered.

There was a loud knock at the front door. Dad went to open it. Mr. Carmody, our neighbor across the hall, stood in the doorway.

"What the heck you got in there, a lion?" Mr. Carmody asked.

"No," said Dad. "A dinosaur."

Mr. Carmody stared at Dad for a moment. Then he left. Dad closed the door. "Zack," said Dad, "this is an emergency. What do we do in an emergency?"

"We call the police," I said. I picked up the phone and dialed the police.

"Seventeenth Precinct, Sergeant Wickroski," said a woman's voice.

"We have a dinosaur in our bathroom," I said. "It's wrecking the place. We need to have somebody come by and take him out of there."

"You have a dino *what* in your bathroom?"

"Saur," I said. The line went dead. "I don't think people want to hear about dinosaurs," I said. I dialed the police again.

"Seventeenth Precinct, Sergeant Wickroski."

"We have an *alligator* in our bathroom," I said. "A very large alligator. It's wrecking the place. We need someone to come take him out of there."

"Do you have a permit to keep an alligator?" asked Sergeant Wickroski. "Because if you don't, you'll have to pay quite a large fine."

I hung up the phone. "Dad, the police say unless we have a permit to keep an alligator we're going to have to pay a large fine."

Dad put his hands over his face. I dialed the fire department.

"Number Two Engine Company, Lieutenant Lerner," said a man's voice.

"Oh, hi," I said. "We have an emergency."

"What kind of emergency? A fire?"

"No. We have...an alligator in our bathroom."

"Is this alligator on fire? We can't help you unless it's on fire."

I hung up the phone. Just then there was a knock on the door.

"Who's there?" Dad asked.

"Professor Fufu," said a voice.

Chapter 8

"Dad, don't open the door!" I whispered.

"Why not?" said Dad.

"Because this Fufu is a really bad guy. Don't let him in! Please!"

Dad frowned at me and started to open the door. I slammed the door in Fufu's face.

"Zack!" Dad shouted. "How dare you be so rude? What's gotten into you?" He opened the door. "I must apologize for my son," said Dad. "I've never seen him behave so rudely. Please come in."

"No, Dad!" I said. "Don't let him in!"

"Zack, you be quiet or you're going to have a time-out!"

"Dad, I'm ten and a half," I said. "Ten-and-a-half-year-olds don't have time-outs."

"What can I do for you, Professor, uh…"

"Fufu. Horatio FuFu. Sir, I'm from the Rosencrantz Museum of Natural History. I had my security guard follow your son home. Yesterday, the boy made a handshake deal to sell me his…animal. And then he took it back."

"Zack, did you make a handshake deal with this man and take it back?"

"Yes, Dad," I said. "Because he wants to—"

"Kind sir," interrupted the Professor, "we don't want this animal at all. That is why we are now willing to pay…four hundred dollars for it."

"Four hundred dollars?" Dad repeated.

"I'm sure you don't care about money. How about *five* hundred dollars?"

"*Five* hundred dollars?" Dad repeated.

"Dad, they only use *dead* animals in their exhibits. He wants to *kill* my poor baby dinosaur."

"Is this true, Professor?"

"Sir, perhaps you're not *familiar* with the Rosencrantz Museum of Natural History? Perhaps you thought we have *live* elephants and *live* whooping cranes and *live* screech owls—trumpeting and whooping and screeching and pooping all over the place? Perhaps you thought I said I was with the Rosencrantz *Zoo*. Is that what you thought?"

I looked at Dad. He sighed.

"All right, Professor," said Dad. "I'm afraid I have to agree with my son. We can't sell you our dinosaur after all."

The Professor's face suddenly turned bright red.

"Do you honestly think you can say no to Professor Horatio Fufu?" he shouted. "Is that what you think?"

"That's what I think," said Dad. "OK, pal. Now I'm going to ask you to leave."

He opened the door. Out in the hall a crowd of neighbors had gathered.

"Do not think you have heard the last of Professor Fufu!" shouted the Professor. "Do not ever be so foolish as to think that!" He stalked out.

The dinosaur roared. A large man with a thick black moustache stepped forward. Oh, no! It was our awful landlord, Mr. Shloffer.

"I can hear the racket you're making all the way downstairs!" he said. "What's going on in there?"

"N-nothing," I said.

"You aren't keeping another one of those awful pets, are you?"

"No sir," said Dad.

"Let me in," said the landlord. "I want to see this for myself."

From the bathroom came the sounds of roaring and the smashing of glass.

"What was *that*?" demanded Mr. Shloffer.

"That was...a buddy of mine," said Dad. "He had too much to drink and got sick in our bathroom. I don't want to have anybody see the way he looks now."

"Oh yeah?" said Mr. Shloffer. "Well then, let me tell you this. Whoever or *what*ever you got in that bathroom, it better be out of there by midnight, *or else*!"

"Or else what?" Dad asked.

"Or else *you're evicted*!"

Chapter 9

We didn't know what else to do, so Dad and I went over to Mrs. Coleman-Levin's apartment. When she opened the door she was wearing a Japanese kimono and bunny slippers.

"Now then," she said, once we'd sat down on the couch. "Why are you so upset?"

"Mrs. Coleman-Levin, you're our last hope," I said. "When we told the police a dinosaur was in our apartment, they hung up on us. When we told them it was an alligator, they said they were going to fine us for not having a license. The fire department won't help us because it isn't on fire…"

"This thing has eaten our shampoo, our bath towels, the bathmat, and the hair dryer," said Dad. "The neighbors think we've got a lion, and the landlord will evict us if it's not gone by midnight."

"My advice," said Mrs. Coleman-Levin, "would be to drive him up to Lake Champlain and plop him in. I believe there are other plesiosaurs in the lake. Your little friend would be among his own kind."

"Lake Champlain is maybe a ten-hour drive from New York," said Dad. "Plus, how are we supposed to get that animal out of there by ourselves? He's as big as a full-grown alligator by now. And just as dangerous. I'm afraid I'd lose fingers if we tried to do it ourselves."

"Have you ever seen Cleve Birwin on TV?" asked Mrs. Coleman-Levin.

"The famous Australian guy?" I said. "The one they call the Alligator Hunter? I love him."

"Cleve's a good friend of mine," she said. "He's in New York for a week before he goes to Africa. He's trying to save a village from a family of poisonous bunny rabbits. I'll call him and see what he recommends."

She picked up the phone and dialed.

"Cleve," she said when somebody answered. "It's Claire Coleman-Levin. Well, it's good to hear yours, too. Cleve, we have a bit of a situation here. A student of mine has a rather large animal shut up in his bathroom. Right. I don't know, I'll ask."

She turned to me and Dad.

"How big would you say the creature is now?" she asked.

"About nine feet when we last looked," I said. "But he's growing fast."

She turned back to the phone.

"About ten feet," she said. "No, not an alligator, Cleve. A plesiosaur. No, Cleve, I'm not kidding. Because I've seen it. Cleve, have you ever known me to kid? All right then. Anyway, I suggested they find some way to get it out of the bathroom and transport it up to Lake Champlain. I don't know, I'll ask."

She turned to me and Dad.

"Is there a window in this bathroom?" she asked.

"Yes," I said. "It's about three feet wide."

"And what floor are you on?"

"The thirtieth floor," I said.

She turned back to the phone.

"They have a window about three feet wide. They live on the thirtieth floor. Well, that's what I was going to suggest."

She turned back to me and Dad.

"Give me your address," she said. "Cleve is going to meet you there with an animal-rescue helicopter."

Chapter 10

"G'day, mate, I'm Cleve Birwin," he said when I opened the door.

I couldn't believe it. Here in our doorway was Cleve Birwin, the most famous alligator hunter in the whole world. Although it was pretty cold out, he was wearing the same khaki shorts and short-sleeved shirt you always see him in on TV.

"Hi, I'm Zack," I said, "and this is my dad."

"G'day, mates," he said. "Well, let me see the little rascal."

I led the way to the bathroom. From inside came the sound of more roaring. I opened the bathroom door. Cleve took a look inside and started chuckling.

"Oh, he's a *beau*-ty!" said Cleve. "A *beau*-ty!"

He walked up to the tub and tried to pet the baby dinosaur on the head. The baby dinosaur snapped at him and almost took his hand off. I didn't think plesiosaurs were supposed to be this fierce. Maybe that's why this one wasn't extinct.

"You're all right, mate," said Cleve. He chuckled again. "He's a little rascal, he is. What a *beau*-ty, though."

"Do you really think it'll be possible to get him out of here through the bathroom window?" Dad asked.

Cleve looked at the window. "Piece of cake, mate," he said.

Just then we heard a terrible racket

outside: THUCK-a THUCK-a THUCK-a THUCK-a THUCK-a. It got louder and louder. Then there were flashing lights right outside our bathroom window.

Cleve looked at his watch. "Right on time," he said. He opened the window and stuck his head out. "G'day, mates!" he shouted to the chopper.

The noise of a helicopter outside our bathroom window was so loud you could barely hear somebody banging on the front door. Barely.

"Dad, somebody's banging on the front door!" I shouted.

"Maybe it's Cleve's people!" he shouted. "Go let them in!"

I went to the front door. "Who's there?" I called.

"What the heck is going on in there?" yelled a voice on the other side of the door. It was the landlord!

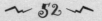

"Is that you, Mr. Shloffer?" I asked.

"You're darned right it is! What is all that noise in there?"

"It's Dad's friend. He's feeling a lot worse. We're taking care of him."

"I don't believe you!" yelled the landlord. "Let me in!"

"Not just yet, Mr. Shloffer," I said. "Dad really doesn't want anybody to see his friend in this condition."

"Tell your father to come to the door!" yelled the landlord.

I raced back to the bathroom. Cleve Birwin had the baby dinosaur in a black canvas sling. The sling was attached to a heavy wire cable that went out the window to the helicopter. Cleve was already pretty bloody. The dinosaur had bitten his ear. It was not a pretty sight. Cleve was carefully— but quickly—easing the dinosaur out the window.

"Soon as this little beauty's in the chopper, you and your dad can follow," Cleve shouted.

"You mean you'd let us come with you to Lake Champlain?" I yelled.

"Sure, if it's OK with your dad."

I turned to Dad.

"It *is* a school night," Dad yelled. "But how many times do we get to take a dinosaur to Lake Champlain?"

Just then I heard a key in the lock of the front door. The door flew open. In came Mr. Shloffer! "Where is he?" the landlord yelled.

I shrugged. He pushed past me and stopped at the bathroom door. All you could see now of the dinosaur was about four feet of tail which was quickly disappearing out the window.

"We called a Medavac helicopter!" I yelled to the landlord. "They're taking him to the hospital!"

"*That's* your father's friend? The one with the tail?"

"You have no idea how sick he is!" shouted my dad.

When we got to Lake Champlain, most of it was covered by this really spooky-looking fog. The pilot brought the chopper down to a foot or two above the water. Then Cleve gently lowered the sling with the baby dinosaur down till it was in the water. The baby dinosaur wriggled out of the sling. He looked up at me, and I swear he cocked his head, as if to say goodbye.

"Goodbye, baby dinosaur!" I called. "I hope you find some friends here!"

"G'day, ya little rascal!" said Cleve.

Then the baby dinosaur swam happily away.

Just before the helicopter pilot took the chopper up for the flight back to New York,

I thought I saw something. "Look, Dad! Right over there!"

"What do you see?" Dad yelled.

"Way back there in the mist! Do you see it?"

Dad looked. So did Cleve.

"I see it, mate!" Cleve shouted. "Sticking out of the water! It looks like the head and neck of an adult plesiosaur! He's a *beau*-ty!"

"It must be Champy!" I shouted.

And then, above the racket of the helicopter, I heard what sounded like the bellowing of a bull. I can't be sure, but I think it was Champy calling hello to his new little friend.

We got back so late, Dad let me skip school the next day. When I went to class the day after that, I told Mrs. Coleman-Levin and all the guys about the trip in the chopper.

"I'm delighted Cleve was able to help you out," said Mrs. Coleman-Levin.

"That is so cool, flying in a chopper," said Spencer. "I would've given anything to fly in a chopper."

"*I* flew in a chopper to Europe once," said Andrew Clancy. "It was so loud I couldn't even hear the movie."

What else happens to Zack?

Find out in

My Grandma,
Major-League Slugger

The White Sox pitcher rolled his eyes. Then he went into his windup a third time. He looked at my eighty-eight-year-old grandma standing at the plate. So did I. I noticed something strange around her hands and arms. A bluish glow. And then the pitcher released the ball.

The ball smoked in. It must have been going ninety miles per hour. Grandma Leah swung with all her might. There was no doubt from the whock of her bat. She'd gotten hold of this one. The ball shot up, up, up into the air. It scattered a flock of pigeons. It streaked out over right field, out over the upper deck. It went over the roof of Comiskey Park and clear out of the stadium.

"About like that?" asked Grandma Leah.

"Just exactly like that," I replied.

THE ZACK FILES™

OUT-OF-THIS-WORLD FAN CLUB!

Looking for even more info on all the strange, otherworldly happenings going on in *The Zack Files*? Get the inside scoop by becoming a member of *The Zack Files* Out-Of-This-World Fan Club! Just send in the form below and we'll send you your *Zack Files* Out-Of-This-World Fan Club kit including an official fan club membership card, a really cool *Zack Files* magnet, and a newsletter featuring excerpts from Zack's upcoming paranormal adventures, supernatural news from around the world, puzzles, and more! And as a member you'll continue to receive the newsletter six times a year! The best part is—it's all free!

- ✂ ---

☐ Yes! I want to check out *The Zack Files* Out-Of-This-World Fan Club!

name: _____ age: _____

address: _____

city/town: _____ state: ____ zip: _____

Send this form to: Penguin Putnam Books for
                      Young Readers
                      Mass Merchandise Marketing
                      Dept. ZACK
                      345 Hudson Street
                      New York, NY 10014